Into the
MOUNTAINS

Prequel to Fire on the Mountain

P.D. SINGER

ROCKY RIDGE BOOKS

El Capitan, Yosemite National Park, California, USA, Circa 1899, by
William Henry Jackson, American Heritage website: Public Domain.

The granite monolith stands 3000 feet (914m) high.

Into the Mountains
Copyright © 2020 by P.D. Singer
Print ISBN 978-1-62622-093-5

First edition Kurt Dreamspinner Press 2012, published as a bonus short with Fire on the Mountain

Published 2020 second edition Kurt, first edition Jake

Rocky Ridge Books
Box 6922
Broomfield, CO 80021
http://RockyRidgeBooks.com

KURT

Granite towered over the two young men, reaching half a mile into the blue of a soft California sky. Pale crystals glittered against the morning, streaked with dark veins of diorite. El Capitan beckoned in the early morning sun; figures could be seen clinging to rock, well beyond arm's reach. No picture Ansel Adams had ever taken compared to the reality of the monoliths jutting out of the earth.

With too much to look at, Kurt Carlson had to focus on this one—"rock" was too small a word. "Monolith" didn't convey the grandeur. He'd stood atop Half Dome, feeling small in the majesty of the Yosemite Valley, where the bones of the world lay bare to men. The thanks had formed a lump in his throat then. Now, at the base of the titan, Kurt could barely swallow.

"If you really wanted to get to the top, we could have hiked up the valley by the falls."

Trust Benji Shaffer to blow a hole in the poetry of the moment. He could be such a fucking killjoy.

"You want to hike, head thataway. I'm going up." Kurt clattered with every movement: carabiners loaded with pitons and hex nuts dangled from his harness. He adjusted the webbing of his equipment rack where it twisted under the loops of blue-and-red climbing rope he wore like bandoliers. He hadn't scrimped and saved for a year for this trip only to hike up the back way.

"So am I, dodo, and I go first. You think I'm going to let you lead on El Capitan?" Benji's rack of climbing hardware made answering metallic noises.

"Fuck yeah, I'm going to lead on El Cap. You think I want to risk coming unzipped again?" Kurt had trusted the protections Benji set on Half Dome last week. His stomach churned; he recalled that near-fall much too vividly. Only two pitons jerked out of the stone when he'd slipped on the traverse, but twenty feet straight down could have turned into twelve hundred feet and an abrupt halt for both of them.

"The rock *flaked*, Kurt. I've never had a placement fail before. It could have happened to you."

"Did happen to me—that's why I'm leading." Kurt didn't want to start this climb by snarling at the guy his life would depend on for the next three days, but he still sported bruises from smashing into an unforgiving chunk of Yosemite National Park. He squinted up the wall. "How'd those Canadian dudes get there ahead of us?" The group of three men had the camp site next to theirs. The five climbers had passed a flask of tequila around the campfire the night before, telling stories of adventures on other big walls.

"By getting up at oh-dark-thirty. You want to wait until they get up another pitch?"

"I don't want to follow them at all. One high-velocity shit

storm per trip is enough." A hazard of being lower on the rock when Nature called. Too bad there was little hope of having the climbing route to themselves. They'd come too close to taking direct hits from the team above.

"Hey, if you'd been looking up, you'd have seen his bare ass."

"There's a time and a place, Benj. This ain't it." There had never been a time or a place with Benji and probably never would be, not that Kurt hadn't nurtured a few dreams of hot nights, lazy mornings, and enough trash-talking to be sure they weren't getting sentimental. *One out of three and don't expect more. He's your roommate, not your lover.* Kurt would take the guff if it meant Benji wasn't bitching about leading. Except Benji never gave up this easily.

"If I'm leading, you get the view."

"Still not the time or the place, jerk-off." Well, at least Benji hadn't broken character. Kurt reached into the pack for the map. "I'm a whole lot more interested in handholds." Not that Benji's rear view wasn't fine, and not like Kurt hadn't taken a good look or five. What, besides his buddy, should he be looking at while holding a rope on belay? Muscles standing out like cords, the intense concentration that Benji'd never given Kurt, his long, lean body pressed against the mountains like a lover—oh yeah, Kurt had no problem keeping his attention on Benji. Not that he'd ever made a move. Benji's friendship had been unwavering since Kurt came out during their senior year—his only reaction was "So now it's official, dude. Did you really think I didn't know?"

Benji'd had the same number of opportunities to look at Kurt, and they'd spent a lot of nights together in tents since Kurt made his announcement. A week climbing in the Wind

River Mountains last summer, a dozen weekends in the Colorado Rockies—and nothing going on but sleep. Hell, Benji could wander across the hall at home, but he never had, and Kurt didn't expect he ever would. If Benji was at all interested, he hid it well behind a parade of girlfriends. Smart, slender, cute and brunet, Benji was a regular chick-magnet and probably got extra boyfriend points for his open-mindedness. Not that Kurt had planned to test Benji's reaction to something a whole lot more up close and personal, but after that little offer.... "Why all of a sudden are you suggesting I look at your ass?"

"Kurt, there are thirty pitches to the top. I'm not going to follow you up every last one of them."

"So you're bribing me?" Benji had a point; following for two-plus days of climbing would wear on an expert, which they both were. Kurt opened the climbing map, a sheaf of sturdy pages bound on hinged rings, flipped to the Salathé Wall page. "I'm leading anything over 5.11, Benji. Look—" He practically shoved the map into his friend's face to keep him from arguing further. "We can start from farther west, and once we're up to Mammoth Terraces, we can slide over the Muir Wall to the Integral and pick up the Nose." That was the big-name route on El Capitan, the one that gave climbers the loudest bragging rights. "If we're fast, we can get past the Canadians."

"There's a chimney on that route. I hate chimneys," Benji grumbled.

"It's a fucking 5.8 in a bunch of 5.11s. You want to lead, you get the chimney. Quit your bitching." Kurt dropped the map with a groan, only to see Benji's brown eyes crinkled up to match his grin. He slapped the map into Benji's chest, huffing at being had.

Actually, Benji would figure out that *he'd* been had, about two pitches from now. The leader got to haul the gear bag up. All their water bottles were full, and while the weight was a self-correcting problem, five gallons would always weigh forty pounds.

Might be Kurt's problem if any of the pulley points Benji rigged were as unstable as the pitons on Half Dome. He didn't need a seventy pound gear bag landing on his head.

"Come on then." Benji grabbed one end of the gear bag, Kurt got the other, and they headed away from the sun to the base of the new route.

Kurt could hear the Canadian climbers calling to one another through the rustle of the breeze in the junipers and lark song. They were probably saying ordinary rope orders like "On belay" and "Belay on," maybe in French, but from down here it sounded more like "Bloop! Bloop!"

"Bloop," Kurt murmured back to them, anxious to be on the rock. They'd already spent too much of this morning sorting gear for the climb. They were only able to come up with two pulleys between them; that would have to be enough. Benji dropped one of his on Half Dome, and they hadn't been able to find it later. Some other climber probably counted it as a gift from heaven.

The first ten pitches were easy enough to free climb, according to the map: nothing over a 5.11 difficulty, no sections so steep or so smooth that they'd need to set equipment for anything but safety. It wouldn't hurt to salvage Benji's pride on this easy stretch—Kurt made a grand "after you, sir" gesture at the granite. Benji dropped his loops of orange leader rope on the ground, and with one end secured to his harness, found handholds and toeholds on the rock.

Kurt didn't have much to do until they had at least one protection point—belaying his partner wouldn't help unless there was something to hold the rope to the rock, so with one eye on Benji, he gave himself over to the beauty of the morning, to the smell of juniper so pervasive as to fade into the background, and to staying warm.

The Salathé Wall was part of the southwestern face of El Capitan, and while they'd be plenty warm, even cooked, when the sun finally fell directly on the rock, right now Kurt was glad for his fleece jacket and nylon twill trousers. He could zip off the lower legs when the sun got around to beating on him, and he'd put on his sunglasses when the light fell more directly on the rock face. Benji, now fifty feet above him, had dressed in shorts. He probably needed to keep moving just to avoid congealing. *About two grams of body fat on that boy. You'd think he'd dress better for conditions.*

Benji was making good time, jamming his fingers and toes into the cracks to crawl up the rock face like a spider up a wall. Kurt held the rope steady, keeping Benji on belay now, feeding out line when Benji called down, "Slack!"

Far above Benji, Kurt could see another team of climbers, who had to have spent the night on the wall. A good night's sleep could be had in a peapod hammock clipped to the bosom of the mountain, if turning over wasn't a high priority. Even if Kurt and Benji spent the night on a ledge, they'd clip in for safety. Getting out of bed on the wrong side would mean a quarter mile drop.

"Off belay!" Benji called down, telling Kurt he'd secured himself. The leader having conquered the first pitch—roughly

150 feet, or the length of the rope—it was now time to begin their exercise in vertical freight handling. A few minutes later, the cry of "Rope!" came down to Kurt, followed by the tumbling green and white flashes of cargo line. After securing the haul bag to the line, Kurt gave it a good hard twitch and prepared to enjoy watching Benji reap the fruit of his demands.

"On belay!" Kurt called up, once the haul bag had stopped moving long enough for Benji to have secured it to a hex nut or a friend. He dipped into his chalk bag and, coating his hands with powder to dry the light sweat that had broken out at the thought of mounting this prize. El Cap—at last. The biggest of the big walls, his to ascend if he could. Not *if*—he could. Would. This mountain had been calling to him since he learned to rappel.

"Belay on!" Benji yelled back. He was anchored, prepared to control a fall. Their technique was designed to protect the moving climber—even when the two pitons had failed last week, Benji kept Kurt from whipping the rope through every carabiner on the way down. But that still didn't mean Kurt was ready to trust their lives to Benji's placements 2,500 feet farther up when they reached the Nose and its 5.13+ overhang.

In fact, maybe they should just stay on the Salathé or cut over to the Muir Wall route. Kurt would rather swap routes than tackle the Nose with a partner in whom he didn't have total confidence. A 5.13 or 5.14 pitch, right on the edge of what could be climbed without an antigravity belt, was no place for distrust.

"Climbing!" Kurt announced his intentions, both hands on

the rock, one foot already searching for a hold with the sticky sole of his shoe.

"Climb!" Benji called back, and Kurt took the first step up on his journey into the sky.

His heart beat a little faster with every foot away from the ground, but.... *Climb, Kurt. Just climb.*

Every small bump or crack in the granite was potentially his friend now, or potentially his foe. Rough stone bit his fingertips, even through the calluses, telling him *hold here, shift there.* Gripping a ledge too small for his entire hand let Kurt pull up another half a body length; a small bump beneath his toe gave leverage enough to push a fraction of the way to the top. The rock, less than a foot away from his nose, was dusty and dry, carrying the faint scent of the rubber-soled shoes of the men who would pit themselves against the monolith.

Keeping his center of balance far enough from the rock to torque his weight into the face, Kurt matched Benji's pace, stopping at each protection point to retrieve the hardware by slipping his nut tool behind each knife-thin rurp or piton, popping it out, and clipping it to a 'biner on his rack. Then upward and onward, man with mountain, to the next pause.

At the top of the first pitch, Kurt shared the hardware back with his climbing partner, who would need it again for the next pitch.

"Too bad your cheap-ass pulley broke." Benji racked the one he'd used to get the gear bag up. A second would reduce the apparent weight of the bag by half, but the bit of useless metal he handed back to Kurt had a broken center pin.

"Not all of us have rich daddies." That was twenty bucks Kurt would have to find before his next climb. "Shouldn't have dropped yours."

"That bag weighs a ton."

"Be careful what you ask for," Kurt told him. "You might get it."

———

Five and a half hours and nine pitches into the day, Kurt was more than ready to stop for lunch and planning. Benji had used his time at belay to scarf some granola bars, but Kurt hadn't loaded his pockets so fully. The apple was a memory from three pitches back. He shared out big chunks from a kosher salami, wanting the protein, fat, salt, and a restful moment to eat it.

"We'll have to make better time than this if we're going to reach the top before the food runs out." Benji wiped sweat off his forehead, leaving a small streak of grease in its stead. The breeze off the rock flipped a strand of brown hair over it.

Calorically dense, wrapperless food, eaten with their hands, wasn't much in the way of cuisine, but it kept the energy up and the haul weight down. Kurt perched against the wall in rest position, one leg tucked under him into his sling to form a seat, the other leg pushing away from the wall. He gnawed his chunk of the garlicky sausage. "Slow leader."

"I am *not* slow." Benji shoved a handful of peanuts and raisins into his mouth.

"We have to average under forty minutes a pitch if we aren't going to run out of daylight before we get to the Grey Ledges." Kurt drank a swig of water from his Nalgene bottle before reaching for his zipper bag of "dessert." He knew, but didn't say, that they were behind that schedule. The chimney Benji pretended to moan about had taken them twenty minutes, but some of the pitches had taken well over an hour to get both men and the gear up.

A fly with delusions of being an airplane, or it wouldn't have been at this altitude, buzzed around them. Maybe a bomber—this sort stung, and Kurt's bare calves looked like a landing strip. He'd zipped off the lower legs of his climbing pants a little too soon.

Benji shooed the fly, which had come to investigate him, back toward Kurt. "Go bite those pretty muscles, fly."

"Don't bite Birdlegs—he's slow enough as it is." Kurt slapped his palms together and made the "plummeting fighter jet" noise for the stunned insect, which might or might not come to before hitting the valley floor an eighth of a mile below.

"Must have been a girl fly." After all these years, Benji still rose to the bait of that nickname.

"You're the one noticing my nice legs." Kurt uncoiled from rest position to tuck the water bottle back into the haul bag. "So you can sit back and admire a while. I'll lead." With the end of the green haul rope dangling from his harness, Kurt braced himself to take the tenth pitch, a 5.7 section where he expected to make up a lot of time. "Belay on."

Benji's brows rumpled behind his dark glasses, but he clipped the orange leader rope to his harness and slung Kurt's blue-and-red auxiliary rope over his shoulder. "On belay. I get to watch your ass for a while."

After the difficulties they'd overcome so far, a 5.7 was practically a walk in the park. Kurt got a good twenty feet up and out of range before he replied, barely creating a break in the conversation. "Enjoy. But Benj—" He mantled onto a ledge an enormous fourteen inches wide. "This is a hell of a time to go bi-curious on me."

———

He'd give Benji some playful crap, but Kurt did turn the thought over in his mind. Was Benji hinting at a change of heart? After four years and enough girlfriends that he could probably only dare call them "honey"? After wrapping the rope around his hips and clipping it into the hex nuts, Kurt called, "Belay off!"

Benji scurried up the rock, retrieving the equipment, which gave Kurt time to study him. *Don't read anything into it —he's just flapping his jaws.* The chill breeze that kissed his legs had to be disappointment. Benji had been a comfort when Kurt had broken up with Drew two years earlier, but the friendly arm around Kurt's shoulders had been only that. Friendly. When Kurt recovered enough to begin to think of it as an arm attached to someone he'd like more from, that arm wasn't there. *Just climb with him, dork. Friends are rare things.*

One pitch above Mammoth Terraces, a shower of pebbles fell on them before the cry of "Rock!" reached them from above. Kurt tipped his face against the wall, but not before a vicious chip stung his forearm, drawing blood that flowed downward. He dared not take his bent fingers away from the small protrusion to inspect the damage. Benji, on belay a hundred feet below, could use an arm to protect himself. The rocks fell into the void, chased by the warning.

"What the fuck?" The only climbers they'd seen on this route when they started this morning had begun their day from fourteen or fifteen pitches up—Kurt and Benji couldn't possibly have caught up with them. Kurt waited out another hail of granite fragments before daring to look up.

The other team wasn't any fourteen pitches ahead now. Two pitches at most, and one man bounced lightly down the wall, his climbing ropes colorful spiderwebs at this distance. He reached his partner, clipped in, and began to tug at his rope. *That's protection already placed if it's on the route, but there's a crack on the next pitch.*

Conversation would be useless at this distance.

The other team passed to one side, rappelling past Kurt's belay spot, traveling downward at several times the speed Benji could make on the way up. "Is everything okay?" Kurt yelled, but he got no answer he could understand. The others passed downward, one at a time.

Benji arrived at the belay point, nursing some bleeding knuckles. "What do you suppose was chasing them?" He stuck his hand in his chalk bag, pulled it out white with pink streaks that stopped growing after a moment.

"Dunno." Kurt offered the water bottle after he'd had a swig. "You want to lead this next one? It's another chimney. 5.8." He checked the route map for advice on equipment. "Be unencumbered" read the note left by the map's first owner.

"No way." Benji's fingers curled protectively around his rack, leaving chalk streaks on his gray T-shirt. Maybe he wasn't kidding about chimneys. "All yours."

"Fine." Kurt shrugged off his rack, secured it to a belay pin he'd driven into the rock, and whipped the ropes into a quick knot attached to his seat harness. He loved the big cracks, loved the rock at his back to brace against, loved lifting himself through the heart of the stone. With freshly chalked hands, he hoisted himself into the slot, traveling upward like an inchworm. He forced his mind to think only about "up" because down was too far to contemplate, protected as he was by only Benji's anchoring below. The tendons in his forearms stood out with the effort of boosting himself, one hand on each side of the chimney. A hundred feet or so to the top, eight inches at a time.

Sweat trickled down his back, to be wiped on the granite every time he leaned back for friction. The crack sheltered him from the worst of the sun—his hands weren't sweating from the heat of the rock. Not questioning, just grateful, Kurt hauled on the cargo line, hearing the jangle of his equipment rack echoing up through the slot. He wanted to secure himself before the gathering wind nudged him off the monolith. He hadn't felt it pick up while he was climbing. With hex nuts and a couple of pitons, he anchored himself to the rock. The sixteen-inch ledge felt like sixteen millimeters until he secured his protection.

Once he raised the equipment bag and called, "On belay!" Kurt had to control the rope by feel. Line of sight didn't show him Benji but did let him know why the other climbers had rappelled down in such a hurry.

They'd been keeping a much better eye on the weather.

The light breeze that carried a hint of chill three pitches down had turned into a fitful gusting. Kurt hadn't felt it inside the slot but was unpleasantly aware of it now. Taking his hand off the rope to find his fleece in the haul bag would betray Benji's trust in his belay—Kurt would endure the chill. He looked out at the sky, grown dark to the west where the afternoon sun hung midway between noon and the horizon. Deep gray thunderheads giving birth to sheets of rain scudded eastward; the sun would disappear in a moment.

"Pick up the pace, Benj!" Kurt bellowed down the slot. He wouldn't pull; unless he wanted to haul his partner up arm over arm, he'd belay but not risk dislodging.

"I'm fucking coming!" held a note of fear—Benji must have looked to the west.

The sun disappeared—Kurt let his sunglasses dangle against his chest. From the rope he'd already let flop downward, he judged Benji to be halfway up the slot. The storm advanced—would it reach them before Benji finished the pitch? Kurt pulled in another arm's length of rope.

The first droplets hit Kurt's cheek, *plip, plip,* but turned to stings, driven by the wind. *Come on, come on!* he implored Benji silently, begging him not to be distracted by the rain. The slot might shield him and the rock from the worst of it.

Kurt had just pulled another five feet of rope through the belay hardware when the rope went taut in his hands. The shock yanked him forward—only the stout webbing of his harness, clipped to the hex nuts and rurps he'd placed, kept him from pitching off the ledge. His heart thunked against his ribcage.

Fuck, it's a long way down.

The bobbing on the end of the rope stopped abruptly— Kurt surmised Benji'd gotten his hands and feet braced against the rock again. Bet he needed fresh shorts. "You okay down there?"

"Rock's wet!" The break in his voice made Benji sound about twelve. "Tight rope!"

Kurt pulled, not that there was a lot of slack. He'd taken up most of it before Benji slipped. The fall couldn't have been more than about six feet, even with the rope's elasticity, but that could still give a guy a case of Elvis-leg. A chimney was a bad place for the shakes. Kurt took up the slack inch by inch as Benji climbed. The wind slapped his face with rain.

His clothes shed some of the water, but even the best superfabrics couldn't deflect the impact of fat drops hurled at twenty miles an hour. Rivulets ran down Kurt's legs into his shoes, and the rope grew slippery. He set another carabiner, glad to see the top of Benji's head, and shortly, the rest of him.

"Guess our pals saw this coming." Benji clipped into the protections Kurt had set. "Fucking weather." His voice still wasn't quite steady.

"Yeah." Kurt could curse the weather, or himself and Benji for not staying alert to the changes, but either way, they weren't climbing any more until the rock dried. Down was a possibility, if they wanted to risk their necks rappelling; up was too damned dangerous. "Bivvy bag time."

"Best eight ounces in the whole damned haul bag." Benji helped Kurt clip the two man shelter in, the wind snapping the fabric viciously and nearly carrying it off the rock like a sail.

"Get in!" Kurt yelled. The raindrops could have been windborne gravel smacking into his bare skin.

He followed Benji a second later, sliding his legs past Benji's ropes. They hadn't unclipped, wouldn't unclip—the bivvy bag resembled a Gore-Tex sandwich bag, not a tent, and certainly wasn't a stable shelf. The ledge was barely wide enough to sit on, but Kurt joined Benji, their legs dangling over, their faces poking out through the ventilation slot. Benji adjusted the fabric to keep the worst of the rain from their faces. Muffled by the fabric, the rain still thudded against them, striking but not soaking.

"Are we having fun yet?"

"Of course we are." Kurt peered under the Gore-Tex,

trying to assess the storm. The sky stretched charcoal past the horizon; lightning split the gray into three parts. "It's an adventure."

"You're letting the water in." Benji leaned back. "Stupid bad weather."

"Chill, dude." Kurt leaned back. "Take a nap or something."

"I want a drink of water, a ham sandwich, and a pillow." Benji shifted his weight, bumping against Kurt with every wiggle.

The bag was small, the ledge was small, and both were rapidly getting smaller.

Eating was a good idea, though. How long had it been since lunch? Kurt could reach the haul bag, but that meant sticking his arm into the storm. He groped around, finding water and a plastic bag of something squishy. Ham and cheese cubes. He groped again, locating some dried fruit and the bag of trail mix. Chocolate would fix what ailed them.

"I said a sandwich." Benji spoke around a cube of pink meat. They'd eaten the last of the bread at breakfast.

"Whiner." Kurt's teeth sank through a piece of the cheap, rubbery cheese. Benji'd be more agreeable once he'd eaten, and in the meantime, Kurt would just count to a thousand. By halves.

The storm beat over them—Kurt risked another peek out. That brought some fresh air in, which they sorely needed. Their own exhalations had moistened the interior of the bivvy bag. Kurt felt like he was trapped in an aquarium.

"We aren't going anywhere tonight." Not with wet rock above and below, and the last light fading.

"So where's that pillow?"

Two hundred twenty-one and a half. Two hundred twenty-two. Two hundred twenty-two and a half... "Just lean on me, okay?" Not that there was much choice.

"If I twist this way, I could stretch my legs out." Benji swung his feet around, pressing against Kurt.

"*You* could?" *Three hundred thirty. Three hundred thirty and a half....*

"We can trade after a while."

"Have to." Getting shoved sideways off the ledge wouldn't happen—Kurt was roped in—but he wasn't comfortable. After twenty minutes that felt like two years, he shrugged against Benji. "Move."

"It's not time yet."

"Look, just slide down. Put your head on my lap." The bag was long enough to permit that, and the shoving would stop.

"Bet you say that to all the boys." Benji shifted as much as the ropes would allow.

"Not hardly, asshole." Kurt had said it to a tiny handful of men in his life. That wasn't funny even as a joke.

This was a lot more comfortable, and Kurt could adjust the ventilation flap, getting more fresh air into the bag without more water. A few drops plopped onto Benji's face, but he didn't say anything. He just wiped them away. His head rolled toward Kurt's knee. He reset himself, but it happened again. And again. Benji groaned and shifted, ending with his face against Kurt's hip.

"Don't get any ideas."

"How about I get hard, and you can brace your head on my dick?" Tired, clammy, getting chilly, and stuck on the side of a rock in the rain, Kurt hadn't had the least thought of anything but comfort.

"Ha ha. Fart and I will kill you."

"You'll already be dead." Kurt tilted his head until he found a position he could probably stay in and shut his eyes. *Four hundred ninety-one. Four hundred ninety-one and a half....*

He woke hours later to full dark, the absence of wind, and cramps. Trying to stretch woke Benji, but he should have been up a long time ago—he was shivering. The bivvy bag offered protection from the wind and rain, but little from the temperature.

"Sit up." Kurt shook Benji's shoulder. "I'll grab the sleeping bags."

Easier said than done—he had to reach out into the haul bag again, and the rain was definitely colder this time. But it would be worth it: the down sleeping bags would insulate even if wet. The inside of the bivvy bag was slick with the moisture they'd exhaled. Kurt flapped some fresh air into the bag, bringing a chill that wracked Benji.

"Get in." *In* was relative—Benji could zip his bag to his hips, and then ropes that led to protection at either side kept the bag spread. Kurt stuck his feet into his own bag, knowing he'd have the same problem, so he spread it wide over, not under, and leaned against Benji's bag. It averaged to one bag per man.

"Cold." Benji's teeth weren't chattering. That was a good sign, but he didn't have a lot of reserves. Kurt pulled him close. Not that he had so much insulation on him, but he outweighed Benji by about twenty pounds of muscle; he could radiate at his buddy. Benji leaned into him, all complaints and razzing frozen silent.

The bag of trail mix was a lump at Kurt's hip after all the

moving around. The chocolate hadn't melted yet. Good. "Eat this."

Benji munched slowly, his hand moving to his mouth under the sleeping bag. Kurt ate some raisins and nuts too, but got a sign of life out of Benji when he reached for another mouthful.

"You're letting the cold in."

"You're hogging the trail mix."

"Here." Shoving some dried fruit and chocolate bits into Kurt's mouth, Benji defended his warmth. At least he was feeding them evenly. Kurt kept his arms around Benji's chest and prevented the edge of the sleeping bag from flapping while he chewed.

"Better?" he asked when the trail mix had disappeared and Benji's shivers had abated.

"Yeah." Benji shifted. "You can let go now."

Kurt pulled back and tried to find a bit of comfort on the ledge, but between the webbing of his climbing harness, the ropes, and the zipper of Benji's bag, whatever tolerable position he had before had disappeared. "My turn to stretch out."

"I'm losing the heat." Benji destroyed the newly found comfort of extended legs.

Kurt considered this as safety, not bitching. Yeah, it was comfort, but also a warning—Benji had to be able to get himself up or down the wall come daylight, and if he was hypothermic, Kurt couldn't rescue him. He could push the body off the ledge and recover it at the base of El Capitan. If Benji whined again, that option might look more attractive.

"If we stretch out together, you'll be warm." But there wasn't enough room on the ledge; Kurt's right shoulder wasn't touching rock.

"I go on top."

"You'll be warmer if I'm on top," Kurt growled.

Benji hunched up into a little ball, his ropes not letting him move away from Kurt.

Okay, there probably was the element of control here. Desperate to straighten his legs again, he'd just have to put up with the Het Dude's definition of masculinity vs. available space. "Oh, all right."

Once they were settled, Kurt toyed with the idea of whispering, "Good night, darling," into Benji's ear, just to give him shit. Funny how he could be tangled up in bedding, hand-fed chocolate, and have a desirable man stretched out on top of him, and it was the least romantic experience of his entire life.

———

"What the hell, Kurt?" Benji woke him with a knee in his thigh, trying to get up and away.

"It's morning wood, stupid." A quick inventory told him what Benji was objecting to. "You've got it too."

"Fuck." The flap opened above Kurt's head, letting in a cold deluge. Benji stepped outside the bivvy. Kurt wished him luck, but the chilly rain would probably deflate him fast enough to take a whizz. When he came back, Kurt took his turn, getting a good look at a sky that wouldn't stop trying to drown them any time soon.

The morning passed in silence, aside from small practical discussions, like "What's for breakfast?" and "How long will it take the rock to dry?" Kurt didn't mind; he had music and stories to entertain himself with inside his own head, enough to drown out Benji's periodic moaning.

Sometime around midafternoon—it had grown brighter outside but the sun was still well disguised behind the clouds—Benji muttered, "An adventure, huh."

"Sure. A true adventure is usually no fun at all while it's happening."

"This certainly sucks, so it qualifies." He lapsed into a momentary silence. "I thought an adventure was when everyone comes back alive."

"You bitch, therefore you live." Kurt turned his back to shut Benji out, as much as he could shut out a man he had to lean against.

———

The Gore-Tex bivvy bag rattled moistly; enough stray rain had dripped in that they had to bail. The bilge came partly from Kurt's insistence on a shower. That meant standing up outside for a while, sluicing himself off while wearing nothing but his climbing harness. He could see Half Dome down the valley, and another dozen monoliths, and could only feel small in the rain that beat on man and rock alike.

Once in the bivvy bag again, Kurt wrinkled his nose at his grimy clothing. He flipped his sleeping bag over his lower body instead of dressing.

"You aren't getting dressed?"

"Some reason why I should?"

"Uh...." Benji eeled out through the opening, letting more rain in. The bivvy bag slanted down under his feet, leaving Kurt fighting for headroom, but he'd just done that to Benji. Grungy shorts and a T-shirt that used to be a different color gray invaded the bag at the end of Benji's arm. Kurt didn't check for underwear.

Headroom and screaming happened all at once—Benji's rope slammed across Kurt's chest. His heart tried to leap out of his ribcage. The ropes pulled taut across him. He couldn't breathe. The ropes crushed him. Fear squeezed his chest harder. The bivvy bag pitched and dented—his pitons held— Benji thrashed for a grip.

"Fuck!" Kurt lunged against all the ropes, fumbling to reach out through the ventilation slot. He grabbed one of Benji's flailing hands. Tendons popped in both their arms— Benji levered himself higher, but couldn't lift backward enough to get his butt back on the ledge. Kurt got a hand into his pit to haul him that last few inches. Benji scrabbled his other hand onto the rock and reverse-mantled himself to safety.

"Watch your step," Kurt said mildly, pretending his chest wasn't heaving. He noted a bleeding scrape showing white and red on Benji's back.

"Now you tell me," Benji panted. He sat still in the rain, scrubbing himself with his hands now and then, until he started to shiver. It might have been chills. Kurt said nothing but took Benji's arm while scrambling backward into the bag and pulled the shelter over them again.

"Cold?" Kurt asked when the shivering didn't stop.

Benji had nothing on but underwear, though he didn't reach for his grubby clothing. "Yeah." He tucked his soggy sleeping bag around his bare legs.

Kurt put his arm around Benji's shoulders and left it there long after the shivering stopped.

The sun went down, and the rain came down. Kurt and

Benji ate again, granola bars and more salami, and the yawning started.

"You gonna use me for a mattress again?" Kurt asked.

"Too lumpy. You can use my leg for a pillow." Benji scooted sideways as far as his ropes allowed, and jammed part of his sleeping bag behind his back.

That was more comfortable, at least for Kurt, who expected to shift around sometime in the dark. If the ripstop nylon on Benji's sleeping bag wasn't so slick, it would be pretty cozy, but his head kept slipping. Benji finally solved the problem by chocking his hand under Kurt's head.

Kurt had nearly drifted off when Benji spoke. "Do you think we're going to die up here?"

"Don't think so. Of boredom, maybe. Or drowning." The sleeping bag was wet beneath Kurt's cheek.

"I thought I was going to die today. When I slipped." His words were so soft as to be nearly lost in the drumming of the rain.

"The belays held." They'd set a dozen pieces of protection for that reason. Kurt knew exactly how it felt to fall and the sudden jerk around his hips that meant he wouldn't slam into the ground at terminal velocity.

"*Your* belays held. Maybe mine wouldn't have." Benji, cocky Benji, admitted he could fail?

"Enough of your protection held that I didn't fall far." Far enough to bring Kurt's heart to his throat.

"But you don't trust me now. And I don't trust me. Kurt, maybe I don't belong up here."

"I trust you enough that I got this far with you." No denying that his trust had slipped—he'd argued about who would lead. "We'll finish the climb. We'll be fine." But that was harder to believe in the dark when his stomach did a flip-flop that felt like falling.

"Easier to believe that when you haven't fallen twice in two days."

"We'll be fine, Benj. Trust me on this one." Nerve was a little hard to come by in the dark in a dinky shelter, but only nerve would get them the rest of the way up, or safely down. Kurt wouldn't admit to doubts now.

He closed his eyes, pressing his cheek tighter to Benji's hip. Turning over—not happening. The hand on his back was a comfort, assurance that he wasn't going to flip out into the void.

Hand on his back. Kurt opened the eye not pressed into the damp sleeping bag.

Benji had to put that hand somewhere. Kurt shut the eye again.

"I do trust you, Kurt." Benji's voice had gone a note deeper than a rope and pitons usually made it. "We take risks together that I wouldn't take with anybody else."

"Yeah." Kurt thought about the next set of risks. "Sleeping here, Benj." But with one of Benji's hands on his back and the other under his head, he wasn't sleeping any time soon.

"We slept together last night."

"And you jumped up like I bit you or something." The bruise on his thigh throbbed with the memory.

"Yeah. That was stupid. Sitting up half the night is stupid too. You aren't really lumpy." The hand that had been a stationary warm presence started travelling up and down Kurt's back.

No, what Kurt was, aside from where the webbing of his climbing harness covered him, was naked. Same for Benji except for some briefs. Climbing harnesses didn't cover much. The sleeping bags still wouldn't zip around their ropes.

And Benji wasn't suggesting they sleep.

"If we were as smart as we are agile, would we be stuck to the side of a mountain in a driving rain?" He could lift that sleeping bag to find out exactly what Benji was suggesting, if the warm hand inching toward his butt wasn't enough hint.

"Then I guess we're stupid in the same way. Kurt"— Benji's hand had reached the curve of Kurt's butt, and he hadn't brushed it away; maybe he was as stupid as his climbing partner—"I thought today, I really thought that I was going to drop a quarter of a mile because I reacted wrong when I woke up. And that I'd spend the entire fall regretting it. But—I don't want to regret it."

"Neither do I." Did it matter how often he'd imagined Benji's mouth under his, their bodies crushed together? There was more than one sort of regrets to be had. The steady patter of rain against the bivvy bag made the space small, squeezing them together.

"And you pulled me back."

"You were tied in. You weren't going to fall." Oh Lord, his body wanted to hear more of what Benji was saying; it was agreeing with every movement of Benji's rock-roughened palm.

"But I couldn't manage alone." Benji's hand came across the crest of Kurt's hip, down, down, ruffling the hairs at Kurt's groin with fingertips. Pressing against Kurt's belly, but not reaching further, though all Benji had to do was lift away a little, to brush the back of his hand against Kurt's cock, which had risen high and hard with the soft words. "Like I can't right now."

Kurt turned toward his climbing partner. In the dark he couldn't see Benji, but he sensed him, heard the slow intake of breath, imagined the question in his eyes. The hand crept an inch higher and stopped. Benji's thumb stroked a little circle around Kurt's navel.

"I trust you, Kurt."

Benji had given Kurt enough shit that he knew what it sounded like—this wasn't it. He knew what the rough fingers combing through his hair meant, and the teasing thumb that played with an almost-opening to his body. His face and Benji's groin had only an open sleeping bag between them; he could brush it away and press against Benji's erection. Benji swayed slightly, bumping against the top of Kurt's head.

"You—you do?" He had to clear his throat to get the words out. Everything Kurt had imagined Benji saying—okay, that he'd thought it would take a Benji on drugs to say—he was hearing now. He sat and swiveled, trying to find Benji's face in the dark. "You do."

Searching blindly, they bumped noses. Days of stubble velcroed their cheeks together, rasping against lips and fingers. Kurt nibbled at Benji's lips, not prepared for the sudden onslaught but catching up fast. Benji's harness jingled, cara-biner against rock, when Kurt ran one hand down his side—clothing that might climb walls by itself hadn't suddenly come back to be in the way. Benji pushed their sleeping bags to one side, creaking their ropes.

Kurt wasn't going to question this. No, he was not going to ask too many questions about why he was suddenly having his fantasies made real. Benji, who could match him pitch for pitch on the biggest walls, who just needed his confidence back, had his hand on Kurt's cock now, while they were tied up on the biggest wall of them all.

El Capitan itself felt like part of this, scraping his back, giving him the barest of spaces to touch Benji—Kurt slipped his hand under the webbing between Benji's legs. The mountain would throw them down if they tried taking the harnesses off—but nothing too vital hid under the straps, and he could push Benji's shorts out of the way. He turned Benji to kneeling, to kiss the soft hairs covering that six-pack. Wiry, strong, sexy, and running his hands down Kurt's back, Benji had declared his trust and now let Kurt touch him. With his arm around Benji's hips and his hand wrapped around that hard cock, Kurt interrupted Benji's moans.

"It's okay if I...?"

"Oh yeah," Benji breathed. "Yeah."

He smelled of rain and rock, of juniper and the sweat of the climb. Benji was granite under soft skin and tasted of the great monolith—he was all of Yosemite in one mouthful. Kurt sucked him down, hooking his fingers into the harness.

And then Benji was the earthquake, doubling over Kurt's shoulder enough to nearly lose his balance, but Kurt steadied him, swallowing, feeling every pulse and spurt against his tongue. Stable in his seated and clipped-in position, Kurt helped Benji sit down again, waiting for more kisses until he'd tensioned Benji's ropes.

"I've wanted to do that for a long time," he mumbled into Benji's mouth, and the words might not have carried over the unrelenting tattoo of the rain. Guiding his companion's hand to his groin, he went hollow inside with the first tentative strokes. Benji held on to Kurt, his head against Kurt's chest, finding a rhythm that faltered from time to time. Nibbling softly at Benji's neck, Kurt encouraged him to keep going, but it stole his breath afresh when Benji stopped to explore, hefting and rolling Kurt's balls or running a finger around his glans and across the slit.

"Please," he wanted to whisper, but held it this first time, knowing Benji looked at but couldn't see what he held. Once, Benji dipped his head, but the contact was a mere breath, and Kurt wouldn't push—there would be time for that. Lots of time back in their apartment in Denver. Not that Kurt would move into Benji's room right off.

"Coming," Kurt found his voice to say, seconds before the climax rocked him. Benji pulled up, clipping Kurt's chin but not delaying the inevitable shudders and waves more than a few seconds. Kurt clutched his companion until it was over, slumping against his tethers when the last spasm passed.

"'S'pose I should have warned you." Benji mopped Kurt's belly with someone's T-shirt; they'd know whose, come daylight.

"It's okay," Kurt reassured him, glad Benji hadn't pulled away. "I just didn't want you catching some spunk in your eye. That really burns." He searched out Benji's mouth for another kiss, just a quick sweep of lips. "I am so wiped for not moving around all day."

A silence that might have been nodding in the dark, then Benji agreed aloud. "I just got rid of one of your lumps."

They stretched out best they could on the tiny ledge. Benji lay down on top again after adjusting their protections. Kurt wiggled under him, searching for what comfort could be had. "I've wanted to do that for so long," he confessed into Benji's ear when they'd stopped moving. "I didn't think you'd ever want to."

"Took me by surprise," Benji muttered back.

"If we can climb tomorrow, we can bivouac at Sous le Toit Ledge if we don't make it all the way to the top. And if we do, it's an hour's walk back to the tent." Kurt finished planning with a nuzzle, scratching his whiskery cheek across the back of Benji's hair. "Lots of room. We'll enjoy it more if we aren't thinking about falling."

"Haven't been thinking of much else." Benji shifted and rattled. Kurt guessed he was checking his harness.

They lay skin to skin between the open sleeping bags, the thudding of the rain lulling them to sleep. Kurt clutched Benji more tightly but more tenderly than he had the night before, and tonight, Benji clutched back.

———

They woke to near silence and, oddly, the croaking of frogs.

"It's stopped raining!" Benji stuck his head out through the bivvy flap. A shower of droplets fell from the edge to douse them, but the sky was blue for a change.

Kurt peeled himself off the shelf more slowly, stiff with the inactivity and Benji's weight atop him for a second night. "About time." He was ready to move, ready to climb, ready to shake out every muscle.

"Warren Harding and his team got stuck for three days in a storm on the first ascent of the Nose. It could have been worse."

"Bet they didn't enjoy the storm as much as we did." Kurt was ready for a good-morning kiss, but Benji was turned, running his hand over the still wet granite. Kurt reached into the haul bag, groping for breakfast. "Not a lot left in here." He shook the haul bag, which was much lighter than when they'd begun their climb. "Yum, cheese. And about half a day's water. We should have been collecting during the storm. We'll be pretty dry by the time we get to the top."

"We're going down."

"Down? Why?"

"Safer."

"If you want to wait until the sun's come around and dried the rock more, we can. We could probably find something to do." Kurt grinned, still hoping for the day's greeting.

"Down. I want off this rock." Benji ignored the stick of cheese Kurt held out, sitting again to roll his sleeping bag, which protruded from the flap. When his shorts pulled out of the flap, stuck in the open zipper of the bag, he slipped them on, quickly refastening the crotch straps of his harness over them. "The sooner, the better. Gah, you've got horrible meat breath."

"So do you, salami boy." If he wanted to descend that bad, Kurt wouldn't press. Safer that way. "Better to bail on an epic climb than complete a mediocre climb."

Dressing against the morning chill, Kurt also rolled and stowed his bag. Shame to be thinking of ending the climb, but if Benji'd lost his nerve....

Rigged, racked, and roped, they were ready to move in less than twenty minutes. Benji still hadn't eaten. "Later. Check my knots."

Kurt already had, just on "better safe than sorry" principles. Benji had to be *really* shaken to have asked.

With his ropes threaded around him, Benji dropped down the side of the monolith, and shortly after, the call of "Off rappel!" floated up. Kurt lowered the gear bag, raised the ropes, and clipped himself in. He enjoyed bouncing down a wall or cliff. Maybe Benji would chill out by the time they got to the bottom.

What had taken them a full day to climb took an hour to descend. One pitch from the valley floor, Kurt spotted a tiny white frog clinging to the granite, its throat pouch expanded. "Benj, look. Little guy wants a mate."

"Stupid place for frogs." Benji adjusted his descender and disappeared.

They walked back to the tent in silence, finding it half collapsed from the storm. Silently they folded it and packed the gear they'd left behind. "Eat something, Benji." Kurt handed him the orange he'd peeled for himself when he saw his partner's hand tremble. Taking it without thanks, Benji ate it and wiped his hands on his shorts.

Packed and laden, Kurt took one long last look at El Capitan, and then had to scurry to catch up with Benji, who marched away, his head down. The hike back to Benji's little silver SUV seemed three times as long as the hike out, even without the weight of the water bottles.

Kurt let the silence linger while Benji drove them over the winding two-lane roads through the mountains and kicked back in the seat for a nap once they crossed the Nevada state line without anything approaching conversation. Kurt woke about twenty miles outside of Tonopah, but Benji didn't say more than "Okay" when Kurt mentioned there was a campground where they could probably get a shower for a buck or two. When Benji dashed into the tiny cubicle, Kurt didn't follow. He wasn't going where he wasn't invited. Benji could stand to relax about fifty percent in order to be merely grumpy. He slept most of the way into Cedar City, his face turned away from Kurt, who steered up the narrow state highway and worried about just how much nerve Benji'd lost in the storm. Enough not to talk again until Kurt pushed the point somewhere on I-70 outside of Grand Junction.

"You're still a good climber, Benj."

They'd swapped off driving at a rest stop a hundred miles earlier, and now Benji's knuckles went white against the gray steering wheel. "I know."

That should have cut off the conversation, but a day and a half of cold shoulder was more than Kurt should have tolerated. "Then why are you brooding? We had an epic. We came back safe to tell about it."

"It's not the climb."

"If it isn't El Capitan, then it's me. Isn't it?" That had been a cold pit in his gut for the last five hundred miles. Only the memory of a warm hand in the dark had kept him from jumping to the worst conclusion right off.

"Yeah. Now shut up."

"No, don't think so. What the hell did I do to deserve being treated like shit?"

"You know." Benji's eyes never left the road.

"No, I don't. What I know is that we had sex, at *your* insistence, and you've been acting like a bear with a sore head ever since. What's the matter, don't I give head as well as every Suzy and Floozy and Poozy you've ever dated?"

"The problem," Benji said without moving his jaw in the slightest, "is that you give head at all."

"What!? You've known I'm gay, like, forever, and it's never been an issue. What did you think gay men do, play Monopoly in bed?"

"I didn't think you were gonna do it to me."

"I didn't think I was either! For fuck's sake, Benji, *you* were the one who came on to *me!*"

"That's not the way I remember it."

"Really? *Really?* Then what was all that about, with you sliding your hands all over me and whispering, 'I trust you, Kurt'?" His righteous anger filled the little truck. "I was keeping my hands to myself until you made it really, really plain that wasn't what you wanted. I did not start anything with you, and I wasn't going to start anything with you."

"You sure as hell finished it!" Benji screamed back.

"I did not do anything you did not explicitly agree to, pal. I fucking *asked* you if it was okay, and you said yes. Twice." Punching the driver at seventy miles an hour was probably a bad idea. Especially on a mountain highway, where the eighteen wheelers would crush them if they didn't hurtle off the blacktop. "And you liked it just fine at the time."

"I could pretend you were someone else in the dark."

"You knew who I was all right. 'I trust you, Kurt'." The words tasted bitter.

"I don't trust you now."

"What! Whyever not? I got your ass up and down that rock, and I didn't do one damned thing you didn't beg for."

"I didn't beg for anything," Benji snarled. "And you said you'd wanted me for a long time—that's what I don't trust."

"I didn't do anything about it. Never was going to do anything about it, not even tell you, until you started playing with my ass." His first reaction had been the right one; he should have kept saying no. Could have spared himself this conversation. He turned away. He couldn't bear to look at the ruins of friendship on Benji's face.

"So why the hell did you?"

"You were saying yes, yes, yes, and I wanted it to be true." *Should have seen this one coming, Kurt, you idiot.* "I didn't think you'd only want me when you were afraid."

"I was not afraid!"

"Sure, sure, you weren't afraid. You didn't question your ability to be on a big wall and you didn't kiss me and you didn't come in my mouth and you didn't jerk me off. Rewrite history, why don't you?"

"I will. I didn't do any of that faggy shit."

"You want to know what's faggy shit? Rock climbing. That's what. Shove that up your idea of manhood. Now you can be proud of your failures."

A horn blasted behind them, making them both jump—Benji'd drifted across lanes, to the displeasure of a big rig. He straightened the wheels before they landed in the Colorado River, which wound back and forth below the highway. Kurt's heart pounded even harder.

"You are so full of shit." Benji gripped the steering wheel like it needed strangling. "Rock climbing isn't gay."

"Ya think? What other sport do you slide your fingers into cracks and be happy to do it? Even greasy cracks. Or jam your fingers into holes? Jam your feet too, although that's a little too kinky for me. And it's perfectly fine to hang out half naked with another guy in some sort of bondage gear and be tied in. I mean up. Hell, you meet another climber and you check out his equipment. You admire his nuts." Kurt twisted every bit of rock climbing lingo to something salacious.

"Hex nuts are aluminum!" If Benji's throat didn't hurt after that yell, it should. "They aren't balls!"

"Your balls are brass. Fuck you for making this out to be my fault." Folding his arms across his chest to keep from slugging Benji, Kurt decided he wasn't going to respond to anything short of an apology. Denver was less than two hundred miles away, and he could close a door on Benji once he got out of the truck. Maybe there'd be something of the friendship to salvage and maybe there wouldn't, but right now all he could think of was that the tiny town of Rifle, just ahead, was too damned far from the city.

Benji hit the town at the speed of wrath, screeching the brakes to bring the little SUV down to the posted limits. Kurt was flung over his seat belt with the deceleration, and then was thrown to the side when Benji did an emergency turn into a small store's parking lot.

"You suck, Kurt." He hit the brake to take up three parking spaces sideways, smashing the gearshift into park.

"You loved every minute of it!"

"Get out!" Before the truck even stopped rocking, Benji was throwing ropes and bags on the parking lot. Kurt bounded out to save his gear.

"I already gave you gas money!" Kurt threw his rope back into the truck and bent for the haul bag.

"Here!" Benji peeled some bills out of his wallet and threw them on the ground. "We're even. We're done. Find the bus station. And I want you moved out by the end of the month." He swept random gear out to one side and leaped back in the truck. The locks *snicked* closed, but Kurt wouldn't dignify Benji's fit by rattling the door. The little silver truck roared out of the parking lot, chased by Kurt's one-fingered salute.

That went well. Kurt slumped, the bags littering the parking lot at his feet. Benji's gear bag had a wheel mark across it. *Guess it's mine now.*

The sixty dollars in gas money that Kurt hastened to

collect before it blew away was seventy percent of what he had in his pocket. It would get him back to Denver, but did he actually give a rat's ass about going? Nothing back there but people who judged, people who threw you out the minute you gave them what they wanted. Fuck that. Was there even anything back at the apartment he cared enough to retrieve? Oh yeah, his skis. Might was well grab his underwear and socks while he was there.

Kurt wasn't so much hungry as dry, but he was standing in front of what had to be the town grocery. While he dragged his possessions into a heap next to the door, a white Ford pick-up truck pulled up and disgorged a stocky middle-aged man in a khaki uniform with a paper in his hand. The man went into the grocery, and in a moment, Kurt followed. No one would steal his stuff, and he needed provisions.

A loaf of bread, a jar of jelly, and another of peanut butter would keep him going for a couple of days. Kurt paid for his meager purchases and then wandered to the bulletin board by the door. One notice, fresher than the others, covered offers for babysitting and a reward for a lost dog.

"Forest Rangers Wanted," Kurt read. "Federal jobs, wilderness life." A fringe of tear-off phone numbers at the bottom still had all the tags. He had a quarter in his pocket; maybe he should indulge his fantasy of never seeing another human face. He detached one flap.

"Interested?" a deep, confident voice inquired from behind him. Kurt turned to find the speaker, the man in khaki, holding a grocery sack.

"Might be." Enough to ask. "What's involved?"

"Patrol duties in the Uncompahgre National Forest. You work six days a week, one day off to come into town for groceries and such, see a movie. You're looking for fires, lost campers, wolf-sign, that sort of thing. I have two-man teams, some on horseback and some in tankers."

He'd just watched a four-year friendship dissolve after two days in a bivvy bag—he wouldn't answer for what would happen after a summer in a truck. No tankers for him. "I can ride."

"No offense, son, but I"m not talking summer-camp trail rides on broken-down nags." The man looked at Kurt with a measure of challenge.

"None taken, sir, but neither am I. My brother-in-law runs the Rocking 9 Ranch in Wyoming. I spent summers in the saddle growing up. When I wasn't running a hay baler. Rode a little rodeo. Fought a couple of grass fires along the way." Kurt knew quite well he didn't look like anybody's idea of a cowboy, not with his blond hair grown down to his shoulders and twenty-four hours of stubble, wearing hi-tech climbing pants with a portion of Half-Dome and El Capitan ground into the knees. "Don't have my own horses, though."

"I think we might be able to find you a pony or two." The challenge had turned to appraisal. "Think you can cope with one person for company, some old sourpuss who speaks four words a day?"

Four might be three too many. "As long as he has his own bivvy bag, I can manage."

"You sure? Most young fellas like you want more elec-tricity than a ranger cabin has, which is none. More night life."

"Been there, done that. If the town has a library, I'm good. Which town, anyway?" Kurt didn't really care, but he needed a shipping address.

"Meeker. And yes, there's a library." The man was openly smiling now. "You are a footloose one, aren't you?"

"Just came off a two week climbing trip in Yosemite. I did have a settled address, but it's time to move on." Benji would probably be only too happy to put his stuff, not that he had much, into storage, or freight it out. His skis might be a shipping problem. "I don't have much besides what I've got with me now."

"There might be some ranger greens with your name on them. What is your name, son?" The man put out his hand. "Harold Mason, but most folks call me Chief."

His grip was warm and strong, but not crushing. Kurt returned it just as firmly. "Pleased to meet you, Chief. I'm Kurt Carlson." This was the most ass-backwards job interview he'd ever had. "Seems a little odd to be recruiting for government work on a community bulletin board, if you don't mind my saying."

"The folks who have the skill set I need don't spend a lot of time on the Internet." Chief smiled widely. "Sure you're good with a crusty old partner and some horses until October?"

"Chief, I like horses a whole lot better than I like people right now." Kurt took a chokehold on his grocery bag. "When do I start?"

JAKE

THE SPRING LEADING UP TO FIRE ON THE MOUNTAIN

I hadn't expected fires would be part of my life this summer. I'd asked a lot of questions and had some thinking to do before accepting the position as a ranger. The flyer I'd found on a liquor store bulletin board led me to talking the the Chief, and he made it pretty clear that anything that happened in my stretch of forest would be my problem.

I hadn't expected a job interview when a bunch of us students spent a weekend up in the mountains in Glenwood Springs, but when a job practically falls into your lap, it needs serious consideration. Even if it means cutting yourself off from civilization. I wasn't sure I could deal with that.

The Chief wanted me to be sure before I said yes. "Can't have you bailing on me mid-season, Jake. Don't start if you don't think you can finish."

My friends found it all funny. "Jake Landon, the new Smoky Bear?" they teased me.

"I don't have that much chest hair," I shot back to the snickering group.

Eight of us had taken the train up to the mountains to swim in the gigantic hot springs-fed pool, kind of a college seniors' "last hurrah" road trip. We'd budgeted the important things first, so we had plenty of beer and tequila and not enough motel rooms. We'd ended up four to a room, and no one had counted noses or couples before we'd set out.

"We'll just politely ignore each other," Tami pronounced, grabbing the room key and disappearing into one room with her fiancé, Paul. Shaun and Lindsay followed them, the door closing on giggles. They'd been seeing each other for a month or so, and I could imagine perfectly well what they'd all have to ignore.

That left Ron, Patsy, Nathan, and me staring stupidly at each other in the motel parking lot.

"Let's see what we've got." Patsy opened the door on two torture racks. Neatly made up to look like double beds, with pillows and bedspreads, but torture racks all the same, no matter how this shook out.

She turned to survey us, her mouth quirked to one side. We were all friends, no hints of dating among us since Patsy and Nathan had tried seeing each other for a few weeks a year ago. Spoiled a good friendship in the process, and strained the entire group while they'd gotten over the fit of lust or whatever it was. I'd spent a couple evenings comforting her and still didn't know what had gone wrong. Now I could practically hear the gears turning in her head.

Patsy threw her backpack down on the bed. "Jake, I hear you snore, so Nathan, sorry, but you are shit out of luck. Ron, you're in with me."

"I do not snore!" Obviously I didn't think, either. Of course she didn't want to share with Nathan, and I couldn't exactly come out and explain why I'd be the most perfect gentleman she'd ever have the fortune, or misfortune, of sharing a bed with. They had no idea I was gay.

I was only moderately clear on this myself. I knew what I wanted and who I liked, but as far as getting it... Never happened. I had no idea how to even open the conversation with a likely date. Or lay. Or... Well, I wasn't thrilled with the idea of getting sweaty with someone I didn't like a lot, and that narrowed down my chances considerably.

"We'll check with Nathan in the morning." The little wench had the nerve to pinch my cheek on her way to the bathroom. She shut the door on us, and I suspected she wanted to have a laughing fit in private.

"The lady has spoken." Ron dropped his pack next to Patsy's, grinning at us. I hoped Patsy knew what she'd let herself in for, even with me and Nathan as chaperones. Or maybe they'd planned it.

I tried not to think about the night during our swim in the hot springs pool, burgers, and the alcohol-fueled talk back at the motel. We'd all be graduating this spring, and what would happen next was very much on our minds.

"I have a job lined up, but it means moving back to Cincinnati," Nathan told us, and took a drink. "I do not want to leave Boulder."

"You'll get over it," Paul said, cuddling Tami a little closer. "You could be moving back to Mama's basement like Shaun here."

"Shut up!" Shaun opened another beer. "So an English major has to look a little harder for a job."

"It's not too late to go to grad school." Lindsay poked him

with her elbow. "Like Jake. Delay the inevitable exposure to the real world."

"I'm going to pharmacy school, brat." I tickled the bottom of her foot, making her jump and spill a few drops of beer. "I'll be Jacob Landon, Pharm.D., four years and a bajillion dollars later. You needn't call me Dr. Landon."

"No, we'll call you Smoky Bear." Tami leaned closer to Paul. "Looked like you were going for a career change and you haven't even started school yet."

"I need something to keep me in Colorado until I achieve residence." My folks had paid for the non-resident tuition, even though I could have gone to Michigan State and had some bucks left over for pharmacy school. The slip with the phone number rested safely in my wallet. "Patrolling a national forest is pretty good proof I'm living in state, and there'd be tuition money saved up. How much could I possibly spend in the middle of the woods?"

"It's what you'd spend in town on a Saturday night that'll keep you broke. You don't buy cheap booze." Patsy reached for the tequila bottle, which sloshed half empty and hadn't come off the bottom shelf.

I'd told myself it was an indulgence just for this trip, but... I think I'd told myself something similar every time I reached to the top shelf for the good stuff. Looking at the glass in my hand, I couldn't recall how many times I'd filled it. Might have been just twice, but maybe it was three times... Or four... Maybe if I drank myself into a stupor, Nathan wouldn't have anything to complain about in the morning. Well, he would, but not that I'd accidentally groped him. Or if I did, I'd have an excuse.

Or if I didn't get totally stupid, I wouldn't do anything

totally stupid. I set the glass down, resolved not to fill it up again.

The bottle was nearly gone and the beers reduced to empties when Tami kicked us out. I'd been careful to keep the consumption down, though Nathan had pounded enough shots that I was more than a little worried that he might hurl before he passed out. I steered him back to our bed and poured him in.

Patsy slurred goodnights at us, clicking off the light before Ron got back from the bathroom. I slid in next to Nathan, hoping comfort and booze would keep him totally oblivious to my presence, because I sure wasn't going to be oblivious to his. I turned my back to him.

"Anyone want to bet what's going on in the other room?" Ron tripped over the end of the bed. For one horrible moment I thought he was going to faceplant into me, but he staggered on to his own bed.

"Don't need to bet, I'm sure we can guess." I clutched my pillow a little tighter, glad that nothing like that was going to happen in here.

Except... Little sounds from the other bed suggested that Ron and Patsy weren't going directly to sleep. Whispers of sheets across flesh, small giggles... Good Lord. If the pillow wasn't such a ratty little thing I would have wrapped it around my head. I tried anyway.

Nathan turned over behind me. Good thing he was asleep. Except he hitched closer to my back, and draped an arm over me. I threw an elbow backward at him, but he snuggled more.

"Kinda sad that you an' me are the only ones not gettin' any," he mumbled into my back.

Real sad, but I didn't need him commiserating with me

about it! I tried elbowing him again, not knowing what was worse, making enough noise to get caught fending him off, or making enough noise that I got caught looking like I wasn't fending him off. "Roll over!" I hissed, but if he heard me, he was ignoring me.

"Warm." So were his lips against the nape of my neck! "I could do ya..."

"Roll over!" I peeled his arm off my chest, intending to roll him myself. I did so not need this. I liked Nathan, and if we didn't have an audience, I might have been more cooperative, or at least asked more questions. To satisfy curiosity if nothing else. Um, he was good-looking, and had a nice body, and I *had* wondered a time or two if he might be interested. But not now, no matter what was going on across the room.

"Is he supposed to roll to you or away from you?" Ron didn't keep his voice down. A *thwap* sounded like Patsy just told him to keep his focus.

"Aren't you supposed to be busy?!" I snarled, using the sound to cover me shoving Nathan across the bed. I used the only excuse I thought would cover us both. "I think he's gonna heave."

"Not gonna heave." Nathan rolled over into a ball facing the other way, at last, leaving me lying on my back and wishing we'd driven, because then I could go sleep in the car.

I stared into the dark, listening to Nathan's aggrieved snorting subside into the evenness of sleep, and to the soft squeaks from across the room. I had an erection so hard it ached, and while I could explain it by what was happening in the other bed, it was all for the man who lay beside me.

"Enjoy yourselves? Patsy inquired the next morning.

"I slept very well, thank you, once the noise died down." I wanted to nip this in the bud. Nathan looked like hell. He didn't need to cope with any snide remarks, and I wasn't going to let her provoke me into any admissions.

"I thought you two were gettin' snuggly over there."

"You thought wrong." I slapped her jeans-clad butt with an open palm.

"Ooohhh! Did I pick wrong last night?" she cooed, rubbing the spot. I hoped it stung.

"Not from the sounds of it," I retorted. "Didn't think you were this crass, Patsy." I shoved my swim trunks and towel into my backpack for the walk down to the train station.

"I'm not the one whacking off from listening to people," she accused me. Unfairly, too.

"Did not! I'm not crude enough to make you listen to me." I was still kind of squicked about them. "Booze and darkness don't equal privacy, you know."

"You didn't like what you were hearing?" Ron came out of the bathroom with his toothbrush.

"Didn't think I was going to be sung to sleep with a sound-track to a porn movie." Honestly, couldn't they have contained themselves?

"If you could go to sleep at all, you must be playing for the other team." Nathan flinched at Ron's gibe. Guess that made some sense of Patsy's complaints, but he didn't need this crap and neither did I.

"What did you think I was gonna do, join in?"

Ron took it wrong, but wasn't misdirection what I'd been using all along? "Hell no, you don't touch me and you don't touch her!" He shoved me sideways, enough to rock me.

"Wouldn't touch either one of you with someone else's dick."

Somehow he didn't find that appeasing. "She's a fine woman!" And he shoved me again.

I shoved him back, and I was enough bigger and stronger that he toppled onto the bed. "Can't please you for wanting or not wanting, can I? And you're damned possessive about a woman who's talking about us like we're interchangeable dildos."

Somewhere in the three-way shouting that followed, Nathan grabbed his backpack and left. I'd follow him, except Ron was slugging me in the gut and Patsy was whaling at me with the ice-bucket.

Tami yelled at us through the open door. "Guys! Guys! Stop it!"

That was enough to get Patsy's attention. She grabbed Ron's arm, which was probably a mistake: she got the blow that was meant for me, and I landed one more punch on him. I left them moaning in each other's arms, which sounded nothing like it had last night.

"See if I ever buy you tequila again!" Or buy any tequila again; I was done with partying if this is what it led to. I grabbed my backpack and shoved out past Tami. "Those two are fucking nuts." Good thing I had my train ticket in my pocket: I wouldn't have to hang around with them, sit with them, or talk with them.

———

I found a cup of coffee, some ice for my eye, and Nathan, all at the train station. He looked marginally better, with a bottle of water in his hand and maybe some aspirin in his stomach. "How are you doing, Nathan?"

He looked at me sideways. "Been better."

"You did have a hell of a lot to drink."

And that was all we ever said about that night.

———

Our group was never the same after that. We were cordial to each other in classes but while I had no problems with Tami, Paul, Shaun, or Lindsay, every time Ron and Patsy came around, it was time for me to leave. We saw Nathan in passing, if at all. I took the slip with the Forest Service's phone number out of my wallet, looking at it long and hard.

I was doing so great with people, maybe a summer in the back-ass of beyond was exactly what I needed. Nobody to cuddle with, no one to fight with, no one to judge. One partner, used to solitude, the Chief assured me when I finally called, and he didn't seem to think I was overeducated and under-qualified for the ranger service. I tested out of four classes, told the University of Colorado where to mail the diploma, and headed for the high country.

———

Find out what happens when Kurt and Jake meet in *Fire on the Mountain*.

KURT AND JAKE

A TASTE OF FIRE ON THE MOUNTAIN

Flames danced on the dead branches low on the lodgepole pine's trunk.

"Damn it! I didn't think the tree would burn!" Kurt looked up from his shoveling to examine the tree at the edge of the woods. It had been smoking only moments ago.

"Stand back. I'll get it." I took hard swings at the tree's trunk with my long-handled axe, hacking away at the side farthest from the small blaze we'd spent the last few hours putting out. The chips flew with each bite of my blade. Some muscle in my lower back screamed in protest. Kurt kept a careful eye on my progress as he threw more dirt on the smoldering remains of the fire. "Better back off. I think it's ready to come down." I wasn't bothering to take the tree down neatly. Time was the bigger concern.

"Push!"

Kurt and I braced our heavy gloves against the bark and heaved, cracking the unchopped part of the trunk, toppling the

48

thirty-foot-high pine to the ground, away from the other trees. It would not take its companions with it to a fiery end.

The tree crashed onto ground already scorched and disturbed, sending up a shower of sparks. We'd shoveled dirt onto burning mountain mahogany and grasses for half the day, trying to contain the fire before it went from heat and smoke to an open blaze. Between digging a firebreak and trying to deal with the burning material, it had been a busy few hours. The tree still bloomed with open flame; putting it out would mean the end of the hardest of the labor. A few minutes of brisk whacking took the crown of the tree off, letting us pull the unburned branches away from the danger zone.

The normally homey scent of flaming wood had a whole different meaning out here.

"So, rookie, what would you rather put out, a lightning fire or a human-caused fire?" Kurt retreated to the shade of the remaining pines to catch his breath.

"Whichever smolders more and burns less." I pulled off my helmet to wipe my forehead. The canteen at my side flapped loosely; I unscrewed the stopper and tipped it to my mouth anyway for the last few drops of water. We had more drinking water back in the truck, but I'd have to hike for it. Kurt took a long swig from his canteen and offered me the rest. The warm, tinny water tasted delicious.

We had left the medium-duty tanker on the one-lane service road that was the only sort of road through most of the Uncompahgre National Forest because we couldn't get it through the trees to the burn area. Half the forest stood miles from roads and had to be patrolled on horseback. The truck got left behind a lot anyway. We had to take what we needed from the equipment bins on the sides and do without the water if we had to hike too far back.

"Yeah, lucky you, that's lightning fires usually, and they outnumber human fires by a wide margin around here." Kurt waved me to follow him to some branches that were emitting puffs of smoke. "What do you think the score is?"

"Don't know." I threw shovelfuls of dirt at the felled tree alongside him. "The other five teams all had one or two fires each when we went into town last, and we haven't been called to respond to one of their blazes." I stomped a smoking branch with the heavy sole of my boot.

"And we haven't had to call anyone in for one of ours. Might be a tie, or we might be winning with three." He stepped back from the burn and unfastened his jacket. "The wind is down. Let's squirt a hundred gallons at it—it's out and it can damn well stay out." We gathered up the shovels and axes and dragged them back to the tanker. More often than not, we'd starve a fire into submission rather than extinguishing it with water in the dry, windy Rocky Mountains.

We'd caught this fire early, still in the "thinking about being a forest fire" stage. It was far enough from the road that trying to put it out with just the water we carried with us in the tank on the back of the truck was hopeless; until the wind dropped, we couldn't have shot it without losing three quarters of the spray. The loss wouldn't have mattered that much if we'd been close enough to a pond or stream to stick the intake nozzle in. Then we could have sucked the stream up and put it to good use without using up water we might need later that day. But no, the fire was far enough from the road and through the trees that we were lucky to have seen it at all, so we fought it the old fashioned way: with dirt, muscle, and cuss words.

Today we won. Losing a battle with fire out here could mean a hundred acres burned, or a thousand, and if it went really bad, it would be a disaster, like the Storm King fire. Firefighters had died battling that one, men and women who loved the wilderness and worked to protect it. I hadn't known any of them personally, but our boss and some of our co-workers had, and they still grieved. The mistakes that happened at Storm King got pounded into us to make us better rangers, to make us more effective firefighters. All this was new enough to me that the responsibility for the land weighed like a stone in my gut. I was glad not to be alone in the mountains for that and a lot of other reasons—Kurt and I made a good team.

Together we dragged the hose out to its full hundred fifty feet through the trees into a small clearing. Kurt jogged back to hit the pump, and I braced myself for the hose going stiff and ornery. The nozzle bucked in my hands as I struggled to aim the stream toward the fire; the water surging through the tube made it hard to control. I had to point it up and over the few trees between me and the burn site, making me glad we'd waited to do it until the wind died down. Kurt returned and steadied the hose from behind me. Four hands could accurately drop the water on the fire site, turning it from a potential disaster into soggy ash.

Together we pumped the water at the forest, and knowing my partner was behind me, helping me, made me feel just a little better. Fire was a scary thing, damned near alive but dangerous, mindless, and able to whup a lone man. The two of us, well, that was another matter today.

"Think that's about a hundred gallons, Kurt?" I'd been trying to estimate the flow just by time passing.

"Just about, Jake. Point it up," he suggested from behind me, "and hang on tight, I'm letting go."

Warned, I was ready for the jolt in the hose when he let go. I wasn't ready for him to sprint out into the private rainstorm I was making, but he'd left his heavy, fire-resistant clothing and helmet back at the truck when he'd gone to start the pump. Now he stood in dusty green utility pants and boots and nothing else, face up to the spray. The water came down on his upturned face, tilted to catch the arcing wetness, his mouth open and eyes closed, arms wide.

The droplets came down on him as he laughed and enjoyed the impromptu shower. The day was warm and the work had been hot, and now he turned from side to side to cool himself. Shallow rivers ran down his tightly muscled chest and arms and soaked his short, blond hair but couldn't make it lie down. Instead, the drops caught the sun, flashing the light back at me, and my breath suddenly came short.

The fire in the woods was out. But now there was a fire in me, and it was already raging out of control.

ABOUT THE AUTHOR

P.D. Singer lives in Colorado with her slightly bemused husband, one proto-adult, and twelve pounds of cats. She's a big believer in research, firsthand if possible, so the reader can be quite certain Pam has skied down a mountain face first, been stepped on by rodeo horses, acquired a potato burn or two, and will never, ever, write a novel that includes skydiving.

When not writing, playing her fiddle, or skiing, she can be found with a book in hand.

Follow the adventures at Pam's website.

Keep current with Pam and the Rocky Ridge gang by joining the newsletter.

ALSO BY P.D. SINGER

Fire on the Mountain (Kurt and Jake)

Snow on the Mountain (Kurt and Jake)

Fall Down the Mountain (Mark and Allan)

Blood on the Mountain (Kurt and Jake)

Return to the Mountain (Gary and Seth)

Coming Out From the Mountains (Kurt and Jake, coming soon)

Running to Him

Spokes

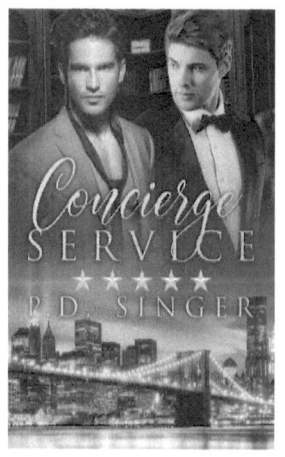

Concierge Service

Returning Soon:

The Rare Event

A New Man

Diving Deep

Get notified of release dates on these and more from Pam, Eden Winters, DH Starr, and the gang by joining the newsletter.

ALSO FROM ROCKY RIDGE BOOKS

The Diversion Series from Eden Winters

Diversion

Collusion

Corruption

Manipulation

Redemption

Reunion

Suspicion

Decision

The Wrestling Series from D.H. Starr

Wrestling With Desire

Wrestling with Love

Wrestling With Passion

Wrestling with Hope

The Dark Angels Series from Z. Allora

With Wings

Tied Together

Finally Fallen

Get news, treats, and tidbits From Pam and the gang by joining the

Rocky Ridge Books newsletter.

www.ingramcontent.com/pod-product-compliance
Lightning Source LLC
Chambersburg PA
CBHW020559130626
46552CB00007B/2957